SECRETS

It wasn't fair, Jessica raged, tears streaming down her face. Enid was going to the fall dance with Ronnie, and she was sure to be named queen. Ronnie was so blind with love that he'd swing a million votes her way.

Jessica sighed. She just *had* to win. If she were queen, Bruce Patman would finally notice her. She'd never wanted anything so badly in her entire life. She'd do anything to make it happen.

Out of the corner of one wet eye, Jessica glimpsed a piece of paper sticking out from under the bed. It looked like a letter.

"Dear Enid," she read with a sudden voracious interest. A smile crept slowly across her features as a plan shaped itself in her mind.

Bantam Books in the Sweet Valley High Series
Ask your bookseller for the books you have miss

SWEET VALLEY HIGH

SECRETS

Written by
Kate William

Created by
FRANCINE PASCAL

BANTAM BOOKS
TORONTO • NEW YORK • LONDON • SYDNEY • AUCKLAND

RL 6, IL age 12 and up

SECRETS

A Bantam Book / November 1983

Sweet Valley High is a trademark of Francine Pascal

Conceived by Francine Pascal

Produced by Cloverdale Press Inc.,
133 Fifth Avenue, New York, N.Y. 10003

Cover art by James Mathewuse

ISBN 0-553-23971-6

Published simultaneously in the United States and Canada

Bantam Books are published by Bantam Books, Inc. Its trademark,
consisting of the words "Bantam Books" and the portrayal of a
rooster, is Registered in U.S. Patent and Trademark Office and
in other countries. Marca Registrada. Bantam Books, Inc., 666
Fifth Avenue, New York, New York 10103.

PRINTED IN THE UNITED STATES OF AMERICA

O   0 9 8 7

SECRETS

One

"My very own sister! How could she do such a hideous thing to me?" Jessica Wakefield fumed.

She shimmied into the dress she was wearing for her date with Tom McKay. Her best friend, Cara Walker, zipped her up, then stepped back and sighed. Jessica was, as usual, too gorgeous for words. Her sun-colored hair shimmered about tanned shoulders left bare by the silky Hawaiian print sun dress that perfectly complemented her blue-green eyes. A bewitching smile on her lovely oval face usually completed the picture of perfection. The only trouble was, she wasn't smiling right now.

"Look at me," Jessica ranted. "I'm an absolute mess! I haven't been able to do a single thing with my hair since this afternoon." She tossed her head in disgust, even though every golden strand seemed to be in place. "Can you imagine— being dunked with every stitch on? How positively humiliating!"

She shuddered at the memory. She'd been tricked—and by her very own twin sister, Elizabeth, who practically always shielded Jessica above and beyond the call of sisterly duty. It was almost too much to be believed. Jessica had been tossed, fully clothed, into the Sweet Valley High pool, the students' annual playful punishment for the author of the "Eyes and Ears" gossip column of the school paper. However, it was Elizabeth who was the columnist, but she'd engineered a mix-up in identity, a trick she'd picked up, no doubt, from Jessica herself.

Cara giggled. "I don't know. I thought you looked kind of cute. Even though you probably deserved to look like a drowned rat. You know, you really *did* have it coming after what you told me you pulled on Liz."

Jessica cut her dead with a glare. "You're lucky we're at your house instead of mine, or I'd really let you have it." Deep down, though, she knew she'd deserved it, too.

"Oh, come on, Jess, you know you really did look kind of sexy. Like Bo Derek in that beach scene in *10*."

A smile pulled at the corners of Jessica's mouth, and the harder she tried to keep a straight

2

face, the worse it got. Finally she collapsed, laughing, onto Cara's bed.

"I did, didn't I? Even so, it *was* humiliating being set up like that." A thought occurred to her, and she clapped a hand over her mouth, sobering instantly. "Oh, Cara, I hope Bruce didn't see me. I'd die!"

She'd been in love with Bruce Patman since her freshman year. He was the most desirable guy in school. Besides being movie-star handsome, he was fabulously rich and drove a terrific black Porsche.

"Just keep thinking of how you'll feel when you're queen of the fall dance," Cara cajoled as she stood in front of the mirror, combing out her own shiny dark hair. "Bruce will be so blinded by your beauty he won't remember anything else."

Jessica wondered if even Cara knew just how badly she wanted that crown. The dance was two weeks away, and she could hardly wait. Bruce had been nominated for king, and it seemed a cinch he would win. None of the other nominees even came close. If she won, too, it would mean reigning at Bruce's side for many of the school-related activities during the semester. It would mean that, finally, Bruce would have to notice her—and, naturally, fall in love with her.

Winning that crown meant everything to her. And when Jessica Wakefield set out to get

3

something, she let nothing and no one stand in her way. Usually it wasn't hard to get what she wanted. With her bewitching looks and beguiling ways, few people ever realized they'd been had by Jessica until it was too late.

Elizabeth Wakefield stared down at the shattered remains of the measuring cup her best friend, Enid Rollins, had just dropped.

"Oh, Liz, I'm sorry!" Enid cried, her eyes filling with tears. "I don't know what happened. It—it just slipped out of my hands!"

Elizabeth hugged her best friend, forgetting the fact that they were both covered in chocolate-chip cookie batter. Enid Rollins was spending the night at the Wakefields', and Elizabeth had initiated Project C.C. Cookie in the hope it would distract Enid from whatever it was she'd been so jumpy about all evening. Actually, Elizabeth had been noticing a nervous edge to Enid's behavior ever since she'd started going with Ronnie Edwards about two months earlier, but she hadn't wanted to pry. She figured Enid would tell her what was bothering her when she was ready. She didn't believe that being best friends with someone entitled her to pry into her friend's private business. But Enid had been in tears when she arrived, too upset even to talk, and things had gone downhill from there. This had gone too far.

"Forget the stupid cup," Elizabeth said. "What's *wrong*, Enid? You don't have to tell me if you don't want to, but just remember I'm your friend. I'm here to help if you need it."

Enid covered her face with her hands. Elizabeth noticed that they were trembling. "Oh, Liz, I'm so afraid!"

"Of *what*?"

"Of losing Ronnie. If he knew the truth about me, he'd hate me. Absolutely *despise* me!"

"How could he possibly hate you?" Elizabeth asked. "The only truth is that you're a fantastic person."

Enid shook her head. "You don't know, Liz. I've even been afraid to tell you. I didn't want you to hate me, either."

"I could never hate you, Enid."

"Maybe not, but I just know Ronnie would if he found out."

"OK, what's this terrible secret?" Elizabeth smiled in an attempt to lighten Enid's misery. "You're really a cat burglar, right? Straight-A student by day, jewel thief by night."

"Come on, Liz, it's not funny." Enid refused to be consoled. A tear trickled down one chocolate-smudged cheek.

"I'm sorry," Elizabeth said. "Really I am. It's just that I can't believe anything you did could be as terrible as all that."

Enid took a deep, shaky breath, then blurted, "Try a police record, then."

"You?" In spite of herself, Elizabeth couldn't help being shocked.

"Yeah, me. Oh, I know what you're thinking. Straight-as-an-arrow Enid. But I wasn't always so straight."

Enid haltingly poured out to her best friend the story that had burdened her for so long. Two years earlier, when her parents were getting divorced, she'd gone a little crazy. She was angry, hurt, upset. She'd drifted in with a bad crowd and gotten involved with a boy named George Warren. They'd gone from drinking to drugs—trying just about everything that came their way.

The situation came to a nightmarish climax the afternoon Enid and George went joyriding in George's GTO—stoned out of their minds—and struck a little boy who was playing near the road. For Enid the whole world stopped moving at that moment. She climbed out of the car as if in slow motion, her knees rubbery. Forever frozen in her memory was the sight of that tiny figure crumpled on the pavement, the horrifying sound of the scream of his mother as she came racing out of her house. Enid stood there as if paralyzed. A voice that didn't seem to be coming from her kept saying, over and over, "I'm sorry. I'm so sorry."

Luckily, the boy wasn't seriously injured. He'd suffered a broken arm and a mild concussion. Enid and George were arrested, but placed on six months' probation and signed into a drug counseling program at Juvenile Hall. Enid emerged from the experience a different person. She'd been shocked into seeing the roller-coaster ride of self-destruction she'd been on, and she'd set about putting her feet on solid ground. She was straight now, with grades to match. She hadn't seen George in two years, since his parents had sent him away to a strict private boarding school.

The whole time she'd been telling her story, Enid was staring down at the kitchen counter, unable to meet Elizabeth's gaze. Now she looked up into a pair of blue-green eyes shining with sympathy. Enid had always thought Elizabeth was pretty—though in a less flashy way than her identical twin sister Jessica—but it was a sparkle that went beyond her all-American good looks, the perfect white teeth, the spun-sunshine hair. Elizabeth was a person who *cared*. She was the first person in whom Enid had been able to confide her terrible secret. Somehow, deep down, she must have known that Elizabeth wouldn't condemn her.

"I'm glad you told me," Elizabeth said. "But it doesn't change a thing. You're still my best friend, and I *still* think you're a fantastic person. Even more fantastic than ever, now that I know what you've been through."

Enid was crying openly now, the tears pouring down her face. Part of it was the sheer relief of being able to unburden herself at last, but mostly she was still in agony over the fear of what would happen if the one person she *didn't* want to know should find out.

She forced a quavery smile. "Tell that to Ronnie. I'll bet he wouldn't think I was so terrific if he knew I'd been lying to him all this time."

"You haven't exactly lied to him," Elizabeth pointed out.

"I haven't exactly told the truth, either."

"Come on, Enid, it's not the most hideous secret in the world, no matter how bad it must have seemed at the time. Besides, it was two years ago—that's practically prehistoric by now."

"Easy for you to say. You don't have any skeletons in your closet."

"If I did, Jessica would've borrowed them." Elizabeth couldn't suppress a tiny smile, thinking of her twin's charming little habit of foraging in her closet whenever she ran out of her own things to wear.

"You wouldn't think it was so funny if you were in danger of losing Todd," Enid insisted.

"I know if it were me, I'd tell Todd. If Ronnie really loves you, he'll understand."

"Oh, Liz, you just don't know!"

Sighing, Enid sank down in the kitchen chair by the window that overlooked the patio. She stared mournfully out over the glassy surface of the lighted pool, shimmering sapphire against the backdrop of darkness. The exact blue of Ronnie's eyes, Enid noted.

"Ronnie's not like Todd," Enid explained. "He expects one hundred percent of my attention. If he knew about George . . ." She stopped, biting her lip.

"What about George? You said yourself you haven't seen him in a couple of years."

"It's true I haven't actually *seen* him. But"— she released a deep sigh—"we write to each other. It's not what you think. I mean, there's nothing going on between us. We're just friends. I started writing to George because he was so mixed-up and unhappy. I wanted him to know it didn't have to be that way forever."

"I think it's nice that you're helping George," Elizabeth said. "There's no reason Ronnie should be jealous over a few friendly letters."

Enid groaned. "You're talking about someone who turns green if I look sideways at another guy by accident. Last week he caught me going over a homework assignment with a guy in my history class. I thought he was going to blow a fuse!"

A tiny alarm went off inside Elizabeth. "But if you explained it just the way you did to me . . ."

"He still wouldn't understand." Enid slumped forward against the table, burying her face in her arms. "I just know I'm going to lose him!"

Elizabeth laid a comforting hand on Enid's

shoulder. "Look at it this way. Nobody knows about these letters except you and me, right?"

"Right."

"So what's got you suddenly so afraid Ronnie will find out?"

"It's George," Enid explained. "In his last letter he said he's coming back to Sweet Valley for a visit in less than two weeks. He's come back before, but this time he wants to see me."

Up in Elizabeth's room Enid dug a sheaf of letters out of her overnight bag. "I brought them along, hoping I'd have the nerve to tell you," she said sheepishly, handing them over to Elizabeth.

Elizabeth read the one on top—George's most recent letter:

Dear Enid,

As you know, I've been keeping pretty busy with exams. They really sock it to us here, which I didn't like at first, but now I'm glad they do. I guess I've been pretty much of a goof-off all my life, so I've had a lot of catching up to do. Studying isn't exactly my idea of having a good time, but in a funny way it really kind of grows on you. I feel better about everything in general, as you know from my other letters. I used to be angry all the time, blaming my parents and everyone else for what was wrong with my life, but I think who I was really mad at was me. I don't want to sound weird or anything, but you helped me see that more than anyone, Enid. You'll never know how much your letters meant to me. I don't mind admitting to you that it was pretty depressing here at first. This is definitely *not* Disneyland. But I won't be here much longer—only until the end of the semester when I'll finally have enough credits to graduate—and the future is looking pretty good. I'm glad to hear things are going so well for you, too. Your last letter was definitely an upper (the only kind I go for these days). I'd really like to see you when I come home this time, but I'll understand if you'd rather not.

Love,
George

P.S. Thanks again for the brownies you sent on my birthday. They disappeared in about two seconds, but they were good while they lasted.

P.P.S. Say hi to my buddy Winston for me.

"I don't know what to do," Enid said when Elizabeth had put the letter down. "I don't want to stop being George's friend, but I *can't* see him. Ronnie would take it all wrong."

"I should think Ronnie would be glad to know how loyal you are to people you care about."

Enid shook her head with stubborn insistence. "It would be the ultimate end. He'd be furious. I'd lose him." She clutched at Elizabeth's arm. "Liz, you've got to promise me you won't tell anyone about the letters. Swear you won't!"

"Cross my heart, hope to die."

Solemnly Elizabeth placed her palm against the nearest thick book at hand, which just happened to be her dictionary. Being a writer, she was never very far from it. Of course, she didn't consider herself an Ernest Hemingway. Not yet, anyway. Right now most of the writing she did was for Sweet Valley High's *Oracle*, for which she was author of the "Eyes and Ears" column.

Elizabeth understood Enid's fear of having something like this leak out. Sweet Valley was still a small town, despite its rapidly growing silicon chip industry. And in small towns, as her father said, rumors had a tendency to multiply like mice in a cornfield.

In many ways Sweet Valley High was the biggest mousetrap of all—the cafeteria, the locker rooms, and the front lawn were favorite centers of communication on every subject from the color of someone's hair to scandals involving drugs and who was fooling around with whom. Most of the gossip was harmless, but occasionally a vicious rumor would spread like wildfire, burning innocent people in the process. Elizabeth recently had been on the receiving end of such a rumor herself, when her eternally two-faced twin was nearly arrested and let the police think she was Elizabeth. The cruel gossip had disturbed Elizabeth greatly, so she was in a better position than most to appreciate Enid's dilemma.

"I swear that if I ever tell about the letters, you can, uh—" Elizabeth grinned as inspiration struck. "You can bury me alive in chocolate-chip cookie batter!"

Enid moaned, holding her stomach. Both girls had eaten so many cookies they were sure they were going to gain at least fifty pounds apiece. But the joke had the desired effect of getting Enid to smile.

"Ugh!" Enid said. "I think I'll just take your word for it. I trust you, Liz, I really do. You're my very best friend."

"I should hope so." Elizabeth laughed, pretending to smother Enid with her pillow. "Who else would invite you to spend the night with the way you snore?"

"I don't snore!" Enid protested, leaping off the bed and dissolving into giggles as she beaned Elizabeth with her own pillow.

"Like a seven forty-seven at takeoff!" came Elizabeth's muffled shriek.

In all the commotion, neither girl noticed as one of George's letters fell to the carpet.

"I give—I give!" Elizabeth gasped at last.

13

"Come on, let's get into bed. We can tell ghost stories. I know a good one about these two teenage girls left all alone in this big creepy house. . . ."

"Elizabeth Wakefield!" Enid cried. "If you tell me one of your ghost stories, I'll never get any sleep. The last time I couldn't sleep for a week."

Elizabeth smelled a challenge—and rose to it. She flicked off the bedside lamp, plunging the room into shadowy darkness.

"It was a dark and stormy night. . . ." she intoned in her creakiest voice.

Enid settled back with a sigh of defeat, secretly glad to get her mind off the real-life fear that was pressing down on her. The thought of losing Ronnie was the worst nightmare she could imagine.

Two

Jessica stared restlessly out the window at the sloping green lawns of Sweet Valley High as Ms. Nora Dalton droned on and on, something to do with conjugating French verbs.

Bore, bored, boring, Jessica conjugated in her mind. It was such a gorgeous day, she wished she were at the beach instead, soaking up the rays in the bronze, wet-look, one-piece she'd bought the week before at Foxy Mama.

Out of the corner of her eye she caught Winston Egbert, seated across the aisle, gazing at her with a goofy, lovesick expression. Yech! Did he have to stare at her like that? Even so, she found herself shifting slightly to a more flattering pose.

"We're ready whenever you are, Jessica."

Jessica whipped about to find herself under the sudden scrutiny of Ms. Dalton, a tall, slender woman in her twenties, whose wide-set hazel eyes regarded her with a hint of knowing amusement.

"Sorry," Jessica said, "I didn't get the question."

"I was just wondering if you might like to let us in on the secret," Ms. Dalton said, her smile widening. She didn't smile often, but when she did, her normally pretty but serious face lit up to spectacular effect.

"Secret?" Jessica echoed, growing distinctly uncomfortable.

"*Oui*. The secret of how you expect to conjugate the verbs I've written on the board if you're not looking at it," she needled in a pleasant voice.

"Mental telepathy!" Winston piped, swooping to her rescue with clownish gallantry. "She's really Wonder Woman in disguise. Hey, Jess, show us how you leap tall buildings in a single bound."

"That's Superman, dummy," Ken Matthews said from the back of the classroom, where he sat with his long legs sprawled across the aisle. Ken also had a tendency to shoot off his mouth whenever the occasion arose. The difference between Ken and Winston was that Ken was tall, blond, gorgeous, and captain of the football team. "And you'll be out of here faster than a speeding bullet if you don't put a lid on it."

"Thank you, Ken," their teacher put in dryly.

"I think we can *all* settle down and get some work done now. Unless," she added, eyes sparkling, "any of you has X-ray vision and can see the answers I have hidden in my desk."

A ripple of laughter greeted this. Ken flashed her one of his thousand-watt grins. It was common knowledge that Ken was hopelessly in love with Ms. Dalton, who had been giving him extra tutoring after class to boost his near-failing grade. Even so, Jessica doubted that Ms. Dalton suspected that Ken had a crush on her.

Teachers could be so *dense* about some things, she thought. *She* was always the first to know it when a guy liked her—as well as the first to take advantage of it when it suited her. Even Winston might come in handy one of these days. The trouble was that right now the only one she really wanted was Bruce Patman, and she might as well live on the moon as far as he was concerned.

Jessica conjured up an image of Bruce—fabulously rich, popular, superstar-handsome Bruce of the ice-blue eyes and coal-black Porsche. If only he would ask her to the fall dance. . . .

Of course, there *was* a way, even if he didn't ask her. Jessica had been nominated for queen. Bruce Patman was up for king. She played out the scenario in her mind. There she would be, utterly ravishing, pretending to look shocked that her name had been chosen. She would glide demurely up to the stage, the merest hint of a tear trembling on her lower lashes—not enough to smudge her eyeliner—as she bowed her head in humble acceptance of the crown.

Naturally, Bruce would be chosen king. He was easily the best-looking boy in school. He would smile at her and take her hand, and the two of them would drift onto the dance floor for a solo dance under the spotlight, as if they were the only two people in the world.

She simply *had* to win. It was her big chance to make Bruce fall in love with her. The dance was only two weeks away, and Jessica was desperate to find a way of winning the crown for sure. She would do anything, absolutely *anything*, to be queen. . . .

She was jolted from her daydream by the harsh jingle of the bell and the mad dash for the door.

Lila Fowler detached herself from the mob, falling in step with Jessica as she made her way toward the lockers, still caught up in the pink haze of her daydream.

"Don't you just *hate* her?" Lila hissed, a scowl twisting her pretty features.

"Who?" Jessica asked.

"Dalton. Who else? Didn't you care that she made a fool of you in front of the entire class?"

"Bite your tongue," Jessica returned blithely. "Nobody makes a fool of me. Least of all a cream puff like Ms. Dalton. Actually, she's not so bad. I kind of like her, even if she *is* a teacher."

Ms. Dalton was one of the newer teachers at Sweet Valley High, so naturally there was a good deal of speculation about her. A lot of it had to do with her being young and pretty—a fact that wasn't lost on the male population of SVH, especially Mr. Roger Collins, faculty adviser for the school paper and resident "hunk" among the male teachers.

Jessica had learned that Ms. Dalton had recently begun dating Lila's divorced father, George Fowler. Anything to do with the Fowlers, one of the richest families in Sweet Valley, was news.

Lila enjoyed the attention, but what she didn't enjoy was the awful *thing* that was going on between her father and Nora Dalton. Jessica suspected that Lila was jealous. She was always vying for his attention, though it seemed as if he never had had enough time for her. Now that Ms. Dalton had entered the picture, he would have even less.

"I don't blame Daddy so much, even if he *is* being incredibly naive," Lila was saying. "After all, she practically threw herself at him. I'm positive she's only after his money."

Jessica wasn't normally in the habit of defending people, but even she thought Lila had gone overboard on the subject.

"Come on, Lila," she cajoled. "I just don't think Ms. Dalton is the man-eater type."

Lila shot her a look of disdain. "They're the worst kind, don't you see? The ones who don't *seem* the type. I mean, look at the way she keeps Ken Matthews dangling, for instance. It's positively disgusting!"

"Ken?" Jessica snorted. "I think you're just jealous because he'll be thinking of Ms. Dalton while he's at the dance with you."

"I am *not* jealous. Just because Ken's taking me to the dance doesn't make him the love of my life. Why should I care if he's got the hots for some other girl?"

"Girl? Lila, honey, Ms. Dalton is practically old enough to be his mother, for heaven's sake!"

"She's twenty-five," Lila replied haughtily. "I asked my father. That makes her exactly nine years older than us."

"It still doesn't explain why she'd be interested in Kenny. I mean, I know he'd probably jump off the Golden Gate Bridge if she asked him to, but—"

"Don't you see?" Lila broke in. She yanked her locker open savagely. "She's too subtle for anything *that* obvious. I'll bet there's a whole lot that we don't know about. I've seen the way she drapes herself across his desk when they're alone in the classroom."

"Really? I hadn't noticed." Jessica peered into the small mirror that was taped to the inside of the locker door as she concentrated on applying a fresh coat of Plum Passion gloss to her lips.

Actually, if Ms. Dalton was having an affair with Ken Matthews, it might even liven things up at school, she thought.

"I wish I could catch her *really* doing something with Ken," Lila muttered. "Then my father'd see what she's like under all that nicey-nice."

"Catch who?" Cara Walker strolled up beside them, her eyes alight with curiosity.

Cara was always looking for fresh gossip. It was one of the reasons she and Jessica were such good friends. Cara was content to let Hurricane Jessica make all the waves, while she followed in her wake, gathering up the debris of gossip that littered her path. With her sleek, dark good looks, Cara was pretty and popular in her own right, though certainly no match for the stunning Jessica—a crucial point in her favor, as far as Jessica was concerned.

"Ms. Dalton," Jessica drawled, forming her mouth into a sexy pout as she looked at herself in the mirror. "Lila's convinced she and Ken Matthews are having some kind of passionate affair."

"*What?*" Cara screeched. This was almost too good to be true. "I don't believe it!"

"Believe it," snapped Lila, slamming her locker shut with an ear-splitting clang.

"You mean, you've actually seen them—"

The rest of Cara's question was swallowed up as the second bell shattered the air. Jessica and

21

Cara both slammed their lockers shut, then locked them.

"Got to rush," said Lila. "I don't want to be late for choir. They're choosing soloists today for the Christmas program. "I'll just die if I don't get lead soprano!"

"Don't worry," Cara assured her. "I overheard Ms. Bellesario in the office telling old Chrome Dome that you were a sure thing."

Lila's brooding expression switched to a look of stunned happiness. First she hugged Cara, then Jessica, who squealed aloud in protest.

"Hey, watch it! You're going to smudge my masterpiece. I want to look absolutely perfect in case I happen to run into you-know-who."

Cara cast Jessica a knowing grin as she waved goodbye to Lila. "You-know-who's initials wouldn't happen to be B.P., by any chance, would they?"

"You've got it." Jessica giggled. "For Beautiful Person."

"Or maybe Black Porsche," Cara joked.

"You have to admit," said Jessica, "there *is* something wildly sexy about a man in a black Porsche—especially if he's six feet plus and has gorgeous blue eyes and is incredibly rich," she added.

Jessica sighed. She'd never wanted anything so badly in her entire life as she wanted to go to the dance with Bruce. It was a new feeling for her. She was used to getting what she wanted—

one way or another. And yet half the time Bruce acted as if he scarcely noticed she was alive, even though she'd done everything she could to get him to notice. Like the time she'd dropped half a ton of books right at his feet in study hall. Bruce had only grinned lazily and without lifting a single finger to help her pick anything up, commented, "Way to go, Wakefield."

This time she wasn't going to let him slide out of her grasp so easily. She had an idea. "Hey, Cara," she said, linking arms with her best friend as they strolled off toward class. "You sit next to Ronnie Edwards in history, don't you?"

"What of it? Got your eye on him, too? I don't blame you. He's not bad-looking."

"He's also head of the dance committee," Jessica put in quickly. "I was just wondering if you would feel him out for me. You know, next time you're talking to him, sort of casually try to influence him to get kids to vote for me."

"Sure thing," said Cara. "But frankly, Jess, I don't see what you're so worried about. I mean, look at the competition, will you? Enid Rollins, for instance. You're about a million times prettier."

Jessica's eyes narrowed at the mention of Enid's name. "Yeah, Enid's a nerd, all right, but she happens to be Ronnie's girlfriend, remember? He could get a lot of people to vote for her."

Cara shrugged. "Who knows? Maybe they'll break up before then."

"No way. Have you seen how they act around each other? You'd think they were joined at the hip!"

"Make that joined at the lip." Cara giggled.

But Jessica was too busy boiling to take notice. She had other reasons for disliking Enid, mainly the fact that lately she seemed to be taking up every spare minute of Elizabeth's time. Time Elizabeth could be spending with her adorable, fun-loving twin sister instead.

"Frankly," Jessica said, "I can't imagine what a cute guy like Ronnie sees in that little creep."

"Liz seems to like her pretty well, too," commented Cara, casting Jessica a sidelong glance.

"Liz!" Jessica snorted in disgust. "Listen, Cara, my sister has absolutely *no* taste when it comes to picking friends. It's positively embarrassing! I mean, what if someone thought it was *me* hanging out with Enid?"

As they turned the corner, Jessica caught sight of Bruce Patman in the crowded corridor. He was loping toward the staircase, looking impossibly gorgeous, as usual, in a pair of off-white cords and a heather-blue sweater that matched his eyes. Her knees went weak as warm Jell-O, and her heart thundered in her ears.

"I've got to go. I'll talk to you later," she tossed distractedly back at Cara, her eyes riveted on the glorious spectacle of Bruce climbing the stairs with the loose-limbed grace of a young lion.

Perfection, Jessica thought, feeling herself grow warm and prickly all over. Bruce was absolute perfection, from his toes to his carelessly tousled dark hair. He looked airbrushed, as if he'd just stepped from the pages of a magazine. Jessica stared after him, hopelessly mesmerized.

"Wait a minute," Cara protested, tugging at her arm. "You never did finish telling me about Ken and Ms. D—"

But Jessica had already forgotten about Ms. Dalton. She had Bruce in her sights, and like a bullet homing toward the target, she was dashing ahead to catch up with him.

Three

"Well, well, if it isn't Little Bo-Peep," drawled Bruce as Jessica fell in step beside him. He raked her over with a flick of his heavy-lidded blue eyes. "Lost any sheep lately?"

Jessica laughed as if it were the funniest joke in the world. Bruce Patman could recite the Gettysburg Address in pig latin and have all the girls in school hanging on his every word.

"I don't know what you're talking about, Bruce," she parried, fluttering her lashes at him. "I'm practically the loneliest girl in the whole school. Would you believe I don't even have a date for the dance yet?"

"I'll bet Egbert would take you. I hear he's really got the hots for you."

Jessica made a disgusted noise. "He's the last

boy on earth I'd want to go with! I mean, honestly, he's like some kind of—of—cartoon!''

Bruce chuckled. "Sure, old Scooby-Doo. Winston's for you, though."

"Oh, he's nice enough, but—well, you *know* what I mean." Jessica rolled her eyes in an expression meant to communicate that Winston was utterly hopeless.

Bruce laughed. "Yeah, I think I do, Jessica."

She felt his gaze travel over her as if sizing her up to see if she was his type. Apparently she met his approval, for his mouth curled up in a slow smile that sent Jessica's pulse pounding out of control. *She* had always known she was Bruce's type. Was he finally getting around to figuring it out as well?

She ran the tip of her tongue over her lips, wondering what it would be like when Bruce got around to kissing her. When, not if. The word "if" simply wasn't part of Jessica's vocabulary.

They were at the top of the stairs, and Jessica cast about wildly for some excuse to keep him from leaving. And then inspiration struck. She reached up, checking to see if her necklace— one of a pair of matching gold lavalieres their parents had given the twins on their sixteenth birthday—was under her sweater. It was.

"Oh!" she gasped. "My necklace! It must have fallen off on the stairs just now. Bruce, you've got to help me find it. My parents would absolutely murder me if I lost it. They practically went into debt for life to get it for me!"

Bruce cast an idle glance down the milling staircase. "I don't see it. But, listen, love, I'm sure it'll turn up. I've got to split. Catch you later." He was gone, leaving Jessica to gape after him in frustrated astonishment.

"Did I hear you say you lost your necklace?" She turned to the voice behind her. There stood Winston Egbert, grinning foolishly and turning red to the tips of his ears.

She sighed. "Uh, yeah, but it's no big deal. I can look for it later."

"Gosh, Jessica, I don't mind helping you look," he gushed. "I'm good at finding things. My friends call me Sherlock Holmes. Once I even found a stamp my brother thought he'd lost out of his collection. You'd never guess in a million years where I found it. Sticking to the bottom of my shoe, that's where! I'll bet that's the last place in the world anyone else would've looked, huh?"

He advanced toward her just as Jessica was trying to step around him. "Ooops, sorry!" Winston blushed an even deeper shade of red. "I didn't mean to step on your toe. Are you OK?"

Jessica winced. Force of habit made her flash a dimpled smile anyway, in spite of her annoyance. "Thanks, Winston, but like I said, it's no big deal. I'm late for class."

"Sure, Jessica," he said, disappointment scrawled all over his face. "I guess I'll see you later, huh?"

The last sight she had as she rushed off down the corridor was of Winston Egbert down on his hands and knees, scouring the stairway for a nonexistent necklace.

Jessica arrived home from school in a black mood. Just when she'd come close to thinking Bruce might be interested in her, he'd done a complete turnabout, practically kicking her in the teeth. Now she was more hopelessly confused about him than ever. She simply *had* to find a way to get him. She remembered how his eyes had traveled over her—he certainly hadn't taken any shortcuts. Jessica warmed, just thinking about it. Maybe there really *was* a chance after all.

"Where's Liz?" she asked her mother, who was home from work early and was washing a head of lettuce.

"I think she's with Enid. Something about an art project. Posters for the dance, I believe."

Trim, tanned Alice Wakefield could easily have been mistaken for the twins' older sister. They shared the same beautiful all-American looks, down to the honey-colored hair that now swished softly about Alice Wakefield's shoulders as she bustled about the spacious, Spanish-tiled kitchen.

"Enid!" Jessica spat with exaggerated scorn. "Ugh! How can any sister of mine hang around with such a creepy little nerd?"

Mrs. Wakefield turned to give Jessica a gently reproving look. "I don't know how you can say that, Jess. Enid's a very nice girl. She and Liz seem to have a lot in common."

"Yeah, that's because she's turning herself into some kind of Liz-clone. It's positively revolting! She's always over here. Doesn't she have a home of her own?"

Alice Wakefield smiled as she patted the lettuce leaves dry. "Sounds like a slight case of the green-eyed monster to me."

"Me? Jealous of Enid Rollins?" Jessica made a gagging sound. "How could any mother say such a hideous thing to her own daughter?"

"Maybe because it's true," her mother suggested pleasantly.

"Mom!"

"Well, Liz *has* been spending a lot of time with Enid. You certainly don't see her as much as you used to."

"It's her business if she wants to associate with creeps, not mine. I mean, if *she* doesn't mind ruining her reputation by running around with that twerp, why should I care?"

"Good question. Honey, would you hand me the potato peeler out of the second drawer? That's it. Did I tell you Steve is coming home and bringing Tricia over for dinner tonight?"

Tricia Martin was her brother Steven's girl-friend. Although he lived in a dorm at the state university which was in a nearby town, he came home a lot, mostly because of Tricia. Most of the time Jessica was horrified that her very own brother was dating a girl from one of the worst families in town. But at the moment she was too preoccupied with thoughts of the social suicide Elizabeth was committing to give it half a second's notice.

"Liz can see who she wants," Jessica repeated. She scowled as she reached into the basket of cherry tomatoes on the sink and popped one into her mouth.

"Right."

"She can make friends with a one-eyed hippopotamus for all I care."

"That's very open-minded of you. Don't eat all the tomatoes, Jess. Save a few for the salad."

"She can hang out with *ten* one-eyed hippos if that's what she wants to do. It's positively none of my business."

"I agree completely."

"If she'd rather be with Enid Rollins than me, why should it bother me? I have tons more friends than Liz does anyway. After all, I was the one who brought Enid home in the first place."

Jessica didn't like to admit it, but it was true. Enid had preferred Elizabeth's company to her own. To Jessica that was simply unforgivable.

She burst into tears. Darn Enid Rollins, she

thought. Darn Bruce Patman, too. She didn't need either of them. Everyone knew that she could get practically anyone to follow her simply by lifting her finger. Was it her fault that Enid and Bruce were blind to her charms?

Alice Wakefield laid a comforting hand on Jessica's shoulder. She was used to such tempests from her younger daughter (younger than Elizabeth by four minutes). From the time she was an infant, they had been as frequent, and usually as short-lived, as clouds passing in front of the sun.

"Don't worry, honey," she said. "No one could ever replace you as far as Liz is concerned."

"I should hope not!" Jessica stormed. "I'm the best friend Lizzie's got!"

"Then what are you getting so worked up about?"

"Nothing. Absolutely *nothing!*" She bit into another tomato and ended up squirting a red jet of juice and seeds down the front of her very favorite pink angora sweater.

"Ruined!" Jessica shrieked. "It's ruined for good!"

Mrs. Wakefield sighed as she handed her daughter the sponge. "Well, in that case, I suppose we could always have it for dinner, since that was the last tomato."

In a rage Jessica fled upstairs. She headed straight for Elizabeth's room and flung herself down on the bed. She preferred her sister's room to her own since it was always much neater. The Hershey Bar was what she called her room, due to its chocolate-colored walls. And it looked, in Elizabeth's immortal words, "like a cross between a mud-wrestling pit and the bargain table at K-Mart."

It wasn't fair, Jessica fumed. Elizabeth was going to the dance with Todd Wilkins. Even Enid had a date—with Ronnie Edwards, who was so blinded by love that as head of the dance committee, he'd probably swing a million votes her way. Ignoring the fact that she could have had her pick from any one of half a dozen boys if she'd wanted, Jessica refused to be consoled.

Then, out of the corner of one wet eye, she glimpsed a piece of paper sticking out from under the bed. It looked like a letter. Being naturally curious—and having absolutely zero scruples when it came to reading other people's mail—she snatched it up.

"Dear Enid," she read with a sudden, voracious interest. "Been so down lately. I can't seem to get my head on straight the way you have. I can't stop thinking about the past and trying to figure out how it all snowballed so quickly. It's like the time we took all those bennies, and before we knew it we were cooking along in the GTO doing eighty or ninety. . . ."

A smile crept slowly across Jessica's features as a plan shaped itself in her mind. She folded the letter, tucking it carefully into the back pocket of her jeans. She would have to put it back, of course, before Elizabeth discovered it was missing, but that was no problem.

Whistling under her breath, Jessica started back downstairs, heading for her father's den, where he kept a small Xerox machine for copying legal documents.

Four

"What is it with Ronnie and Enid?" Todd asked. "Are they having some kind of a fight?"

Todd and Elizabeth spoke in hushed tones while waiting for Ronnie and Enid to return to their seats with the popcorn. The two couples often double-dated, and the Valley Cinema was a favorite hangout. They'd always had a good time together in the past, but that night Elizabeth, too, noticed that something was off.

"Ronnie does seem to be acting strange," she admitted.

She didn't want him to know how truly worried she was for Enid, worried that somehow Ronnie might have found out her secret. She'd promised Enid she wouldn't tell, and that meant Todd, too, even though he was her boyfriend and she felt closer to him than anyone else.

Elizabeth looked over at Todd, more grateful than ever that he was hers—despite all the devious plots Jessica had cooked up in the beginning to keep them apart. Jessica had wanted him for herself, and Elizabeth could certainly see why. Todd was one of the best-looking boys at Sweet Valley High, besides being its hottest basketball star. He was tall and lean, with brown hair that curled down over his forehead and the kind of deep, coffee-colored eyes you could drown in. But the best thing about him was that he didn't give a darn whether he was popular or not. He was friendly with whomever he wanted to be friendly with, and he avoided people he considered snobs, no matter how popular they might be. In that way he and Elizabeth were alike. And she knew that she could tell him anything that was bothering her and he would have understood.

"Did you notice he didn't hold her hand during the movie?" Todd noted, giving Elizabeth's hand a reassuring squeeze. "Seemed kind of funny, since he's usually all over her."

She nodded. "Poor Enid. She really looked upset."

"I just hope Ronnie's not on one of his jealousy trips again. Remember the time he got mad at her for talking to that guy at Guido's?"

"All she was trying to do was make sure he didn't put anchovies on her pizza."

"It's crazy," Todd said, shaking his head. "If you love someone, you should trust him. Or her. Seems pretty dumb to get all worked up over nothing when you could be having a good time."

"Like us, you mean?" Elizabeth leaned close and brushed the side of his neck with her lips.

Todd kissed her softly in response.

She felt a tightening in her chest as she imagined what it would be like to lose Todd. Her heart went out to Enid, who had a thousand times more reason to worry.

"I hope Enid's all right," she said when she spotted Ronnie making his way down the aisle— alone. "Maybe I should go up and check."

She found Enid in the bathroom, dabbing at her eyes with a paper towel.

"Enid, what's wrong?" Elizabeth asked.

Enid shook her head. "I—I don't know. Ronnie's been acting like a different person all night. It's like he's a million miles away." Her eyes held a tortured expression. "Oh, Liz, do you think he knows?"

"Maybe it's something else," Elizabeth suggested not too hopefully. "A family problem. You mentioned his parents were divorced. . . ."

"Because his mother was fooling around with another man," Enid supplied bitterly.

"I'm sure it's not easy for him, living alone with just his father. Maybe they're not getting

37

along. You really should talk to him, Enid. It might be something *he's* afraid to tell you."

"Yeah, like he wants to break up, only he's afraid I won't give him back his frat pin."

"Ronnie wouldn't do that. He loves you." But even as she said it, Elizabeth didn't feel very sure.

"To Ronnie, loving someone means absolute faithfulness," Enid said. "If he suspected for one second that I'd been writing to George, it would be the end. He'd never forgive me."

Anyone that inflexible didn't deserve someone as nice as Enid, Elizabeth thought.

"Don't worry," she said. "I'm the only one who knows about the letters. And even if he found out about the other stuff, it all happened way before you met him. He can't hold that against you, can he? It wouldn't be fair."

"Who ever said love was fair?" asked Enid, blowing loudly into a tissue.

She quickly fixed her makeup, then gave her shiny brown hair such a vigorous brushing that it flew up around her head in a crackle of electricity. She squared her shoulders as she gave her reflection a final inspection.

"Maybe I'm just imagining things," she said in a small voice. "Maybe Ronnie's just in a bad mood."

Elizabeth hoped she was right.

* * *

Riding home after they'd dropped off Elizabeth and Todd, Enid felt as if the gap between the bucket seats of Ronnie's Toyota had suddenly become the Continental Divide. She'd been hoping his silence was due to the fact that he felt uncomfortable about talking in front of Elizabeth and Todd, but he was acting just as distant now that they were gone.

"Where are we going?" she asked him when they passed the turnoff for her street.

"I thought we could park for a while," Ronnie replied in a neutral tone.

Glancing at his profile, silhouetted against the amber glow of a streetlight, Enid felt a surge of hope. He wanted to be with her after all! She longed to reach over and thread her fingers through the curly, reddish-brown hair at the nape of his neck, but she resisted the impulse. Even though it was clear he wanted to be with her, she still sensed something was wrong.

Ronnie found a place up on Miller's Point, a favorite Sweet Valley parking spot that overlooked the town. Already there were four or five other cars parked, and judging from the steaminess of their windows, they'd been there awhile.

Ronnie didn't waste any time. He lunged at Enid immediately after he switched off the engine, kissing her so roughly she was left gasping for breath.

"Hey, what's the big hurry?" She attempted

to make light of it, even though she was trembling when she'd finally managed to untangle herself from his crushing embrace.

Enid felt a growing sense of alarm. Ronnie had never acted like this before! Usually he was gentle, never pushing things beyond the limits she set. Tonight he was acting—uncontrollable. Something was terribly wrong.

"Sorry," he muttered. He sat back and began fiddling with the tape deck.

Loud, throbbing rock music filled the car. Usually, he chose something soft and romantic, but this evening he obviously wasn't in that sort of mood.

"Ronnie—what is it?" she blurted. "What's wrong?"

He drummed his fingers nervously against the steering wheel, unable to meet her eyes. "Uh, well, I didn't want to tell you, but it's about the dance. I, uh—"

Enid felt as if her heart were suspended in midair. "What about the dance?"

"I'm not sure I'll be able to make it. You see, I might have to work for my dad that night. He's going out of town, and he really needs someone to look after the store."

"Gee, Ronnie, that's too bad." Enid felt sick.

Ronnie's father owned a small all-night supermarket, but Enid knew he could have called upon any one of half a dozen people to replace him. Ronnie hadn't even bothered to come up